A JAR FULL OF JOYS

A Jar Full of Joys
Edited & Compiled by Namita Das
Print Edition

First Published in India in 2021
Inkfeathers Publishing
New Delhi 110095

ISBN 978-81-950205-3-9

www.inkfeathers.com

A JAR FULL OF JOYS

Edited & Compiled by

Namita Das

Inkfeathers Publishing

DISCLAIMER

The anthology "A Jar Full of Joys" is a collection of 13 stories by 13 authors who belong to different parts of the globe. The anthology editor and the publisher have edited the content provided by the co-authors to enhance the experience for readers and make it free of plagiarism as much as possible. Unless otherwise indicated, all the names, characters, objects, businesses, places, events, incidents- whether physical/non-physical, real/unreal, tangible/ intangible in whatsoever description used in this book are either the product of the author's imagination or used in a fictitious manner. Any resemblance to actual persons, objects, entities, living or dead, or actual events is purely coincidental. The stories published in this book are solely owned by their respective authors and are no way intended to hurt anyone's religious, political, spiritual, brand, personal or fanatic beliefs and/or faith, whatsoever.

In case, any sort of plagiarism is detected in the stories within this anthology or in case of any complaints or grievances or objections, neither the anthology editor, nor the publisher are to be held responsible for any such claims. The author(s) who holds the rights to the story, shall be held responsible, whatsoever.

CO-AUTHORS

Anand Sharan

Rashi Sadhu

Deepti L. Sharma

Neha Prashar Verma

Nivedita Karmaran

Priyanka Sahi

Vishakha Naware

Susan Bowman

Shaikh Abdul Wasee

Vaishali Chandorkar Chitale

Anita Gonsalves

Arundhati Sahoo

Swathi Umashankar

CONTENTS

MEET THE EDITOR

Namita Das

Namita Das is an engineer who used to write software programs and codes but her heart was always set on writing creatively. So, she stroked her pen and started blogging. A quick visit to her website www.penitratherkeyit.com is a stress buster with snazzy humorous writing pieces that keep readers abreast with the latest happenings.

She is the author of the hilarious book 'It's Punny… Oops, I mean Funny' and its sequel, a bonus shortie 'Happily Technically, Ever After!'

EDITOR'S NOTE

I have authored two books, co-authored multiple anthologies, scribbled hundreds of blog articles and now this happens to be my first inscription officially as an Anthology Editor. This is momentous for me in my writing journey because every first holds a notable place in our lives.

Let me tell you, the why and how about the book. One fine day, I just stumbled upon this project offer at Inkfeathers Publishing, an opportunity to design a book. Whatever theme in this world I could choose from and get a chance to network with brilliant budding authors. I mostly blogged humour and so it was my obvious genre choice and idea for the anthology too.

I got on the bus ride in search of some similar minds like mine, seldom did I know that humour was not everyone's piece of cake. After a prolonged search for months, I found these 13 gems of authors who shared the same school of thought – spreading happiness and smiles.

I wish my wonderful co-authors' huge success in their authoring journey.

Without taking any more time let's jump on to read the beautiful stories which will surely make you smile.

P.S. - Beware of where you read it. You may end up getting some stares and awkward nods as some pieces can make you giggle, a lot.

A JAR FULL OF JOYS

1

Passing Through Time

by Anand Sharan

My son turned five months old and he has already started recognizing faces and understanding our commands and certain speech. He is an outcome of our continuous effort and sleepless nights when the two hormones mingle with each other in the correct proportion and at the right timing. Of course, we can talk about the role of testosterone and estrogen but first, let me introduce myself. I am Andy, married to Simmi, who loves and cares for her hubby that is me, more than anything in the world. (Psstt… I was lying, she is not listening to me now, so let me tell you the truth, she only cares for the baby and I am just a helper dad now taking her thrashings all day on *daddy-ing* the baby. Sigh!).

Now let me introduce you to the mini-boss of the house. Aarya, the tiny tot who is discovering the new world of excitement and mischievousness.

Aarya has learned a lot of new gestures with each passing day. He just imitates us, our actions, and our words. I don't know if that's good but it is always mesmerizing to see him following us in some way or another. One such gesture is to greet people by pulling their spectacles and throwing them down before they can react, it's already on the floor near your feet about to crackle beneath your weight, if you aren't alert.

The best part is the innocent smile which he always flashes on any abrupt and new sound made by us like knock-knock, tongue twisters, mouth farting.

"Is it a big task to bring up a child?" Jyoti, my cousin questioned during a video call. Jyoti got married recently and left her single and freedom life to a joint family arena.

"Yeah." Simmi nodded over the video call while cleaning Aarya's bums with wet wipes.

Moving inside the video frame I added, "Jyoti, you know Simmi always asks me to get these particular brands of wipes which are never available in the nearby shopping complex."

Once I had just returned from the office and Simmi demanded to restock the depleting stocks of wipes and nappies. I had to wander across the other part of the town which took me 30 minutes to reach there only to bring that one brand of nappies. To add to my misery, my scooty suddenly broke down midway which I had to tow on foot for about one KM to the nearby service station. That brand of nappy was nothing but a gimmick that Simmi got from one of our neighbours who has used it for her baby several years ago. Her nosiness doesn't end here, she often comes to our house for babysitting sessions.

"Jyoti," I added further. "Never go by the rhetoric speeches of people around you. Always listen to genuine advice and save yourself from these kinds of situations."

Ah! I have another one that happened yesterday with Aarya's gestures. He was playing around and jumping on my lap. I was working from home and had to take an urgent call on office Teams (Microsoft). Somehow the camera got switched on, (thanks to Aarya's fiddling on the laptop keypad). Unaware, I was still holding Aarya in my lap while working on the code. As the call was about to end, one of my teammates commented.

"Good Job Anand for the patient babysitting and you look good too."

That's when I realized that I was live streaming, as everyone in the group chuckled. To my misery, my manager added, "I will certainly give feedback to Mr Bill Gates to add a child lock feature to Microsoft Teams application to cover such use cases in their next upgrade plans.

The other day, there was a Eureka moment in my house. I was busy assembling my office, connecting chargers, and USBs when a sudden shriek startled me. It came from the next room. I quickly leapt through the entangled cables and reached there only to find Simmi and her parents clapping excitedly. Papa claimed he heard Aarya mumble a few words like dada and mamma. With astonishment, they started calling relatives over video call and everyone tried their luck to get him to call them like Uncle, Aunty, Niece, blah blah blah but with got no success.

After some time, they realized that it was only a vocal and sound modulation that the Aarya was imitating. It reminded me of the cuckoo, my pet rooster back in the countryside years ago who would start cockerel in a very unusual way when he was in the transition phase from a lovely chick to a young rooster.

I am sure, at that point, Aarya must be thinking that these guys must have become crazy and they wasted his time the whole day with the same chunk of words. Aarya's mind would be like "I could have learned some new vocabulary on food and other stuff which could have helped me getting my favourite chocolates later."

With the time passing by, Aarya also grew, in weight and he was a few inches longer than what he was a month earlier. Some of his clothes were not fitting with his growing bones.

A week ago, we got a parcel from Simmi's Aunt. It looked very old dated and must have been stuck somewhere for a month and a half. However, were already intimated about the arriving courier well in advance. We unpacked the parcel and found a soft toy and some items of clothing for Aarya. Aunt must have been tracking the courier details and somehow find out that we have received the courier.

The phone rang and as expected it was Aunt. "Did you like it? We purchased it from a very popular and branded showroom, so you must try and send us the pics. Can't wait to see Aarya in those dresses." The aunt was exhilarated.

Simmi looked at me while I continued unpacking the sealed envelope, gesturing to me what are gonna we do with this stuff. It was above a month the parcel had left another city and our Aunt seems to have picked clothes were based on her size assumptions. Guess, what! It was undersized and would not fit Aarya.

Aunty was so excited that she would call every day to check if Aarya is wearing the clothes. We knew the phone will ring again and we will have to answer her inquiries, so we gave it a try. After the bath, we started putting on the new clothes on Aarya but with each try, there was a cacophony in the room as if he pleaded with us to stop this torture of stuffing him inside small clothes. He was feeling discomfort and started a tantrum. I must be hallucinating but I heard him say, "What is all this Dad, that too of old-fashioned Aunty's choice? Now I will choose my clothes."

We thought of a mischievous trick to play with Aunty. We dressed Aarya in another suit and wrapped this new outfit on him so that it would look like he is wearing it. After clicking pictures and adding a few filters and edits, we sent the pictures to Aunty. That is when finally, the calls stopped.

"Your baby will look best in this kurta set," said one shopkeeper while I was hunting for a good dress for the Annaprashan (first food ceremony). I wonder how the shopkeeper decides which is best and which is worst for my baby when they are supposed to sell all the items in their shop. It reminded me of a watermelon seller who would set up his big temporary stall in summers with hundreds of melons stacked together in a pattern. Whenever you ask for the sweetest watermelon, he will start tapping on multiple pieces and after a series of rejections, he would pick one and hand it over to you. Does it mean that he was going to discard the rejected melons and throw them again to the fields? The answer is a big No. It was nothing but a business strategy to emulate as an esteemed customer.

With a child, comes along a lot of accessories like bottles, spoons, holders, cloth stands, prams, etc. "Purchase Walker-234 from First cry shop only" suggested our neighbour randomly when he met in the lift and started explaining the features. He mimicked like a door-to-door salesman reading a product brochure for the advertisement for his new product.

I pondered what if I go for another brand since there are many sellers ready to deliver similar products through e-commerce portals. A few days later I realized that the shop he referred us for purchase belonged to his close friend. He was just helping him grow his business. I understand, nothing wrong with that only if I could get a good neighbour discount.

"S & R initial letters would be best for your baby." claimed a random old lady from the ancestral village. This was communicated to us by our maternal Aunt before just before we planned the naming Ceremony. My internal search engine started hitting my brain's information base and several names started sprouting in my mind. Nevertheless, Indian cinema goes on par with one's thinking. My mind narrowed down two popular names 'Ranchordas' and 'Shahastrabuddhi'.

'Hmm,' I questioned myself, 'Am I deciding the future profession of my child by giving such fancy names? Will he be the one who can solve the issues of physics related to displacement motion and power formulas? Or will he be a hard-core mathematician solving the mysteries of mathematics and equations?'

"Hope you are capturing all the moments of your growing child". A statement surfaced from my cousin who has just celebrated the first birthday of his son. He is a pro in still photography and editing, he often writes articles on the camera lens and other accessories. Once he almost persuaded me to purchase a top-class Nikon still camera which was so costly that I had to plan to get a personal loan. It could have fulfilled the KPI of the tele callers who often call me from different numbers and offers personal loans at an attractive rate of interest. Luckily, I again disappointed the tele calling agencies and restricted myself from being trapped in the loan overhead.

"Why don't you put up a CCTV camera in your baby's room. It will act as dual-purpose - 'surveillance' and 'all moments' capture." I suggested my cousin last time he called me and to my surprise he readily accepted it. I gave a double pat on my shoulder congratulating myself on the success to get the low-cost solution having been implemented to an extravagant person.

Another day passed with few new learnings of fatherhood where I learned to make bottled milk. Proportion is the word that keeps on moving around my ears all the time these days. Even the ratio proportion in mathematics was not so complex as the proportion of milk in water or water in milk.

One day, Simmi asked me to prepare a bottle of formula milk. I did my best to follow precision when she suddenly popped inside the kitchen and started yelling. Why? Because I had added milk powder first and poured water next. Oh! And there came another lecture. "Andy, don't you understand the meaning of proportion? Can't you read the instructions on the milk powder box? It should always be 120 ml water first and then four spoons of milk powder over that. And why are you holding the bottle in your hand? It must be always kept on a plain surface at the level to correctly measure the volume."

Before I could clarify, she again started "I know what you are going to tell me to know that your measurement is correct."

After a few minutes of getting lashed left and right and taking a lecture. I felt like I was in the school cadet training camp taking an oath of the well-being of my country with no grievances and a sense of pride just that right here, the country was replaced by a baby.

I am trying to recall when I had taken that kind of pledge, one was the last time during the school days during the morning prayers, and then the next was during the marriage rituals for seven lives together with Simmi. Vowing in front of fire, family, and relatives that I will take care of Simmi and never let her down in any circumstances.

I was lost in thoughts reminiscing the wedding memories and baby Aarya giggled with a dimple on one of the cheeks. As if he can understand all those conversations between his mother and me. Seems I am raising a mamma's boy who has already teamed up with his mother and learning a hundred ways of mischief. Leaving me to my misery that I can write a book named "The Plight of an innocent but caring Daddy".

2

50 Rs. Is 50 Rs.

by Rashi Sadhu

This story is a real-life incident that happened with my grandparents, which they tell and retell every time we meet. Whenever I narrate this story to anyone, it brings giggles and smiles to the listeners' faces.

My grandfather B.K Munshi was a very admirable man, a school Principal in a county called Pampore, Srinagar, J&K. He used to carry a charming smile on his glowing face with his delightful nature which caught everyone's attention. Half-bald with a short moustache, a religious dotted red tilak on his forehead would be his unique personality description. He was a pious soul with deep faith in God. Very humorous in person but also strict about discipline, punctuality, and diligent follower of neatness. He was a dignified personality known amongst his peer group and in his county.

My grandmother Mohini, a beautiful woman with curly and dense hair, cat eyes, even now when she's nearly eighty years old she looks gorgeous. She has a strong character, a religious mind, and is self-disciplined. Blessed with four daughters, she has dedicated her life to taking care of the family and home wholeheartedly with a smiling face always. When I was young, she taught me that it is good to be brave, follow your heart, and never give up no matter how many difficulties discourage you. She was married at a very young age, in a big joint family which made her mature and responsible from an early age. Then carrying the entire burden of household work solely on her shoulders kept her so occupied that she hardly got time to think about herself. She has always been an over-caring person not only for her husband but for everybody at home. Such a beautiful soul and a true inspiration for everybody especially for other women in the vicinity.

Both grandpa and grandma being very occupied in their responsibilities, hardly got to mingle or spend quality time with each other. For this very reason, my grandfather planned to go out once a year for a week to a religious place (Tulmul) and enjoy the local fair too, it would be their only trip as a couple as well as devotion to God, a double benefit. This was their 'big' event of the year. This was the closest they ever got to have a vacation or to get rejuvenated.

There was a horse cart, an antique one, seen every year at that county fair, it used to take visitors on a tour around the place. It was unique looking, beautifully covered, and decorated that would give each guest the royal treatment. My grandpa being a fun person was eager to take the ride once.

Each year Grandpa would tell Grandma, "I want to ride in that Antique Horse Cart carriage."

And each year she'd say, "I know, but that cart ride costs fifty rupees, and fifty rupees is *fifty rupees*, not a small amount."

Well, I can't call her a miser, she was just focused on spending each penny wisely. She has always given priority to needs rather than desires as she had faced financially tough times in her life so she valued money differently. This Grandma's denial for a cart ride would happen every year. Still, Grandpa would request one ride without fail every year.

Once again, (I don't remember the exact year) Grandpa and Grandma went to the fair as usual, and Grandpa said, "Honey, I'm seventy-one years old now. If I don't get on to that horse cart carriage ride this year, I may never get another chance."

Grandma replied, "My hubby, that horse cart ride costs fifty rupees. And fifty rupees is *fifty rupees.*"

The coachman of that horse cart carriage overheard them and said, "Folks, I've seen you come here year after year. I know you've been wanting to ride in my antique horse cart. I also know that money is pretty important to you, and you don't part with it lightly. I'll make you a deal. I'll take you both up for a ride. If you can both keep quiet for the entire ride, and not say a word, I won't charge you. But if you say even one word, it'll cost you fifty rupees."

Grandpa and Grandma agreed. They got on to the horse cart finally and moved ahead. The coachman started gently but picked up pace after 500 meters. He did all kinds of twists, turns, rolls, and dives, but he didn't hear a beep from either of them. He tried his fastest bumpy roll and it was still quiet at the back. Both Grandma's and Grandpa's eyes were closed, holding each other's hands firmly. The strong winds had pushed their heads against the rubber black seat banging into it multiple times giving them a headache. Grandma's curly hair was flying and messed up. Their heart was beating rapidly as if it would pop out.

As the ride ended, the coachman looked back and asked Grandpa, "I don't believe it, Mr Munshi, I did everything I could think of to get you to yell, but you didn't."

Grandpa replied, "Well, I wanted to scream my lungs out. My wife almost fell out of the cart and I wanted to bellow, then I remembered," He paused and looked at Grandma with a smirk. "But, fifty rupees is *fifty rupees.*"

And all of them laughed out loud!

3

Chit-Cheats

by Deepti L. Sharma

"Hey, you! Yes, grandfather, I am talking to you. Where are you going with your bag in hand? That's an examination hall and you can carry nothing except your admit card and your writing material. Come, keep this bag out here."

The septuagenarian looked at Mrs. Singh in a bewildered manner.

"The bag has my tiffin box in it. My food…"

"…cannot be carried into the exam hall. Come, come, you can leave your lunch safely here. I'll let you have it once the exam is over."

"You won't eat it?" he asked suspiciously.

"I promise you, I won't."

With great reluctance, the old man kept his bag at the place indicated and moved into the hall. One of the peons stationed there hastened to check his admit card and to lead him to his seat.

"Sushma, can you come here for a moment?" Mrs. Sen called out to Mrs. Singh.

Mrs. Sushma Singh walked over to the exam hall door where her friend and colleague Mrs. Geeta Sen stood beckoning to her.

"Sushma, what could a 'hath batti' be? A Maulviji sitting in my exam room wants it."

"A hath batti? Beats me. It could mean a beacon or flambeau type of thing, but why does he want it? Does he wish to set the school on fire? Wait, I'll come with you and talk to him."

Mrs. Singh offered to do this as Mrs. Sen was a little less fluent in Hindi.

"Yes, Maulviji, what do you need a hath batti for?"

She addressed an old Muslim cleric with a henna-dyed beard sitting with an utter look of dejection on his seat by the window.

"Madam, I cannot see well here. I need some extra lighting. Could I get a hath batti?"

"Maulviji, this seat is near the window. You are getting all the possible light here. I don't have a hath batti and I could not have given you one even if I had it because I don't know what it is. I have one option for you – would you like me to move your desk and chair in the field outside? You will be able to see well in the bright sunlight."

Maulviji brightened visibly, like the aforementioned sunlight.

"But there is one condition. There will be a guard right near you and you will not be able to…ahem, you get it?"

The brightened Maulviji metamorphosed into the dejected one.

"No, no. I am fine here. I think I shall manage."

Mrs. Singh heaved a sigh of relief and came back to her room. Almost all the candidates were seated by now as the examination was due to begin in a minute or two. She duly began her job of personally checking each candidate's admit card and signing their answer sheets.

The second candidate she went to was sitting quite perplexed. He looked up at her and said, "There's something wrong here. There is a printing mistake."

"Where, show me?"

"Here. They have written 6 upside-down." He was pointing at the number 9 printed on the answer sheet where it formed a part of the day's date.

Mrs. Singh looked hard at the old man, wondering if he was under the effect of opium or toddy. It seemed not. He looked innocent of intoxication but genuinely confused. Finally, she said, "It's not an upside-down 6. It's 9. Nau in Hindi."

"Oh! Is that so? Must be, must be if you say so. Ha-ha-ha daughter, my knowledge of English is very poor. Forgive me."

Mrs. Singh proceeded on her way without comment. Truth be told, she had no idea what comment to make.

After ignoring an old woman who was openly cheating from a thick book that was a kunji - a guide book - she reached an old man with streaming eyes. His spectacles were no good to him, for he was peering deeply into a chit hidden in his palms but not able to decipher the hints. Finally, he gave up the pretence of not cheating and raised the chit high above him to catch the light properly.

"Goodness me! What do you wish for, grandpa? To make me lose my job? Oh-ho, cheat grandpa, cheat, but so openly? If the inspection team catches you, both of us will be gone."

"Sorry, daughter. But what do I do? No light here for these old eyes of mine to catch the small lettering. It is entirely my son's fault. He has written the answers in such small, cramped handwriting that I cannot make out a thing. Let me just walk over to that window with it so that I can see properly.

"Certainly not! Do whatever you want but remain seated and don't raise that chit in the air again.

Wiping her forehead, Mrs. Singh went on with the formality of matching faces with photographs on the admit card and signing on the answer sheets.

A few seats down the column, once more she came upon an old man sitting quite immobile. His answer sheet was blank and he had not even written his name.

"What happened, grandpa? Any problem where you need my help?"

"I was wondering where I would sleep after the exam. You see, to reach here on time I had to leave my village at 1.30 am this morning and I could not catch up with my sleep.

"You want to take the test now or to go to sleep?"

"Test.

"Then begin writing. Once the test is over, you can go to the government rest-house on the school campus and sleep as much as you want. Okay?"

"They will let me sleep there?"

"Certainly."

"Will there be a mattress on the bed they will give me?"

"Definitely."

"Will there be clean sheets?"

"Surely."

The candidate looked satisfied. He uncapped his pen and began to scribble his name on the answer sheet. With this, too, chalked as a successfully solved problem, Mrs. Singh proceeded.

The door of the examination room was suddenly thrown open by a peon. "Madam, the inspection team is here."

Mrs. Singh was instantly alert. "On your marks, everyone! Hide your chits and your books and kunjis. Don't be caught or you are gone."

There was a sudden flurry of activity. The old woman who had been cheating from a book instantly pushed it under her butt and sat over it. One old man plunged his chit into his mouth and began to chew it fast, like betel leaves. Three women pushed their chits deep inside their blouses. Another old man got so rattled by the sudden tension that he simply threw the chit away from him. The chit went and landed beside another candidate. This man was relatively younger. He was dark and bearded and had the height and build of a professional wrestler. He wore a red vermilion mark on his forehead and a garland of marigolds reposed on his chest as if he had been to a temple just before the exam. The chit fell right by his feet.

With a roar, he rose and walked over to the old man who had thrown the chit. "You little rascal," said he as he collared the old fellow. "I shall throttle the life out of you. Trying to land your crimes at my door, huh? Let's see how you do it now."

There was much whining and apologizing from the old man. There was also a good deal of intervening and pacifying on the part of Mrs. Singh and the peons.

By the time the case was settled, the first member of the inspection team had already trickled into the room. "What is happening here? Why are all of you aggregated there?"

"Nothing sir, nothing at all. Just a trifling matter. Please come in."

The examination room became a model of perfection for the next few minutes. Whatever ruffled feathers the inspection team member had had, were smoothened adroitly. He had entered belligerently, but by the time he had had his cup of tea and a few biscuits, he was ready to beam. Inside of thirty minutes, this agent of the government was on his way out of the room. So were the chits and books – not out of the room, by a long shot, but surely out of their places of concealment.

Mrs. Singh came out for a much-needed whiff of fresh air. She found one rustic elderly man walking hastily towards her. He was a bit too late for the examination. In his haste, all the chits that he had managed to hide on his person were fluttering about him. From his socks, from the folds of his dhoti, from the pockets of his shirt, chits were coming out and doing a merry dance about him, like a flurry of white gnats. He was snapping and clutching at them in an agitated manner.

Mrs. Singh bit her lip in a bid to hide her amusement. Then she shook her head at herself. The guards employed by the school administration to control cheating were sitting on stools near where the old man was and was laughing heartily at the spectacle he made. Some were even clutching at the many chits and passing them on to him, along with their rude comments.

About two hours later, the exam had been wrapped up and Mrs. Sen came out of her examination room to meet Mrs.

Singh again. "I don't know Hindi very well, but isn't there an axiom that goes… 'Andher Nagri…' or something like that?"

Mrs. Singh sighed. "There is. It goes, 'Andher Nagri Chaupat Raja'. A dolt king ruling over a chaotic kingdom. I get your meaning, dear."

"I wish they would assign others to invigilate these exams."

The Maulviji came out of Mrs. Sen's examination hall.

"Madamji, I kept trying to remember throughout the test an English name for hath batti. And I have just got it. It is a torch. You know, the one that runs on batteries and gives light?" Extremely pleased with himself, he smiled and nodded at the two ladies and walked out.

The candidate, whose tiffin box had not been permitted in the examination hall, came belligerently to Mrs. Singh as if expecting that she had cleaned it off every scrap of food. She handed over his lunch to him before he could make a statement. The candidate intent on catching up with his sleep was right behind him. To him, too, Mrs. Singh did not allow speaking up and wordlessly pointed out the location of the government rest-house. Both old men walked out.

"Did you look at all those examinees?" Mrs. Sen asked. "They look fossilized. How can they still be in service? Most of them must be a hundred at least.

"Oh well, you know what. Hiding their ages is the prerogative of only two categories of people – film stars and government employees."

They both shook amused heads at each other and watched as the candidates filed out of the door one by one. The door bore a banner. It read:

IN-SERVICE EXAMINATION FOR RUPEES 500/- HIKE IN THE SALARIES OF GOVERNMENT VILLAGE SCHOOL TEACHERS

4

The Vegetarian Poachers

by Neha Prashar Verma

It was a beautiful Saturday morning and a complete silence engulfed the girls' hostel. Asking the reason will be as futile as asking the reason for sunrise daily. Of course, all girls were dozing off after Friday night ritual of central dance party. Absenting yourself from that party in the hostel compound will put you in a league of unpardonable offenders since the seniors had ordered juniors to make sure that everyone is in attendance.

Neha, Achla (aka Achu) & Shubhi (aka Shubs) - the three nocturnal mavericks of the senior-most batch would wake up directly to grace the lunch layout in mess. Unfortunately for them, their roommates were morning people, specially Shefali (aka Shefu) - Achu's roomie. But this Saturday, she had dropped her usual chore of kicking everyone out of bed. This was a special day for her. Her parents had shortlisted a boy for her and had fixed her meeting with him. The boy was performing an unbelievable feat of travelling from Lucknow to Noida for the date.

Shefu was all charms and giggles ever since the news was broken to her. She spent the last week preparing her dress, matching accessories, purse, perfumes, and the list was endless. After all, the guy coming over was presented as perfect marriage material by her parents after shooting down many others.

The almirah door gave out an unearthly creak, desperately demanding a greasing of rusty hinges. The sound shook up Achla. She let out a volley of curses on Shefu in despair, being robbed of a perfect siesta. She showered some choicest expletives as she got up rubbing her red eyes. As she looked at Shefu standing in front of her in a bright pink suit, she could not control herself and fell back on the bed in laughter, clutching her belly. The demonic laughter sent out shock waves like a nuclear blast to all three rooms in the cubicle – enough to awaken the remaining occupants.

Within seconds Neha, Meenakshi (aka Mints), Shubs, and Bhagyashree (aka Rani) scrambled from the beds and rushed to the room, and burst out in hysteric laughter, joining Achu. They had never seen any one of them in typical heavy work Indian attire before. Even Shefu couldn't stop herself and joined the gang.

Once everyone realized the reason behind Shefu's sudden transformation, the gang decided to send an escort party with her. Neha, Mints, and Achu were nominated as volunteers for the gallant action. Although this was in serious contravention to orders of Shefu's parents – who asked her to go alone, rightly sensing the naughty creatures amongst whom their daughter lived. But then you can't stop friends, can you?

The planning was done to the minutest of details, that they will travel in separate autos. They will enter the mall a few seconds behind Shefu and will shadow the potential couple around, trying to assess and grade the groom-to-be on various attributes listed by the group together. It was also decided that they will message Shefu from Achu's cell phone from time to time to give their report so that Shefu could moderate her talks according to the feedback. It looked like a perfect but untested plan.

The gang moved out to the designated rendezvous unanimously decided by Shefu i.e., Delhi Darbar restaurant in Centre Stage Mall, Noida. They reached well before time to avoid being surprised. As Shefu waited near the entrance, the rest of the girls occupied a table near the one which was booked for the duo.

Bang at the right time, the boy Vishal appeared. He greeted Shefu and escorted her inside, without realizing that people were assessing even his walk. Ah! The girl gang was impressed by the looks of the boy. They messaged Shefu, '*Munda mast hai, What a guy! Handsome, great body, lean waist and best is his Lucknowi attitude*'.

Shefu read the message and gave big smile to Vishal. Soon the waiter came and placed menu cards on the table. Vishal without opening the menu asked for a coffee for himself and sat relaxed. The observant girls took note of this turn-down moment as the boy didn't have the courtesy to ask the lady first. Out went the message, '*No. This guy will keep you hungry whole life*'.

Shefu read and gave a scared expression, followed by a witty smile to Vishal. The girls shook their heads in disbelief when she ordered a huge sandwich and tea for herself. The poor girl had skipped her breakfast in the excitement of the date and was starving now.

'*Eat less, you greedy cow*', messaged Achu. Free of any guilt, the trio had already ordered aloo parathas with copious quantities of butter and were chomping off like hungry goats, greasing their fingers. Of course, there were no potential grooms with them to impress.

Vishal's coffee came first but he waited for Shefu's order to be served and then offered Shefu to start first. Neha got flattered on that and messaged Shefu while gulping the one-foot long lassi glass, '*Not that bad indeed, he is a gentleman*'. This again brought a wide smile to Shefu's face.

The potential couple continued talking and the trio kept an eagle's eye on every movement of Vishal while guzzling down hot gulab jamuns. Suddenly Shefu said something and Vishal laughed out loud – loud enough to make some heads turn. Achu noticed the awkwardness generated by the 'careless' gesture and shot off, '*He is a maniac; he will embarrass you every time you go out.*' Shefu's smile suddenly lost a few kilowatts of radiance. They continued talking and seemed to be comfortable with each other sans reactions to the messages.

Then suddenly, as if out of mischief, Vishal shot off a series of questions in a rapid-fire. There was a series of ayes and noes from Shefu followed by a clear blush of confusion and guilt on her face. And then, to her surprise, he looked around the restaurant and asked in a teasing tone, loud enough for the girls to hear, "So how many of your friends are judging me right now?"

Shefu looked at him with the widest eyes full of horror. Mints tried to hide behind the bowl of gulab jamun, rolling her eyes, "Bugger is Sherlock Holmes!"

Shefu was adequately confused now and gave a side glance in the trio's direction. They all wanted to drown in the leftover gulab jamun juice right there. They made a futile attempt to pretend to not knowing anything.

Vishal commented, "See this is unfair. I am alone and three poachers are stalking this innocent pest."

Shefu was dumbfounded. She started fiddling around with the corner of her dupatta and said, "They are not poaching, they are all vegetarians."

"Dumbo Shefu…" Achu murmured. There was a full one-minute silence till Shefu realized that she had connected poachers and vegetarians. She burst out in a laugh and sure enough, Vishal joined her. No one was bothered about other people now. Both looked at the girl's gang and waved at them.

It has now been eight years that Shefu and Vishal are married and on many evenings their kids demand Neha massi and Mints massi to narrate the Delhi Darbar incident; while Shefu still blushes, Vishal hears the story every time in apt attention. Of course, the massis are still called 'vegetarian poachers' in the house.

5

A Wasted Night

by Nivedita Karmaran

That was the same annoying sound that Kajal heard almost every day. The mixer grinder was switched on in the kitchen. She heard its distinct sound in her sleep. She turned around in her bed, placing another pillow over her head to block the sound. Whirr it went once, Kajal groaned hoping it was the last.

As if her wish was granted, everything around her was quiet except for a dog barking in the far distance. She smiled despite her eyes being closed. She was on the brink of falling asleep again. She felt herself drifting deeper and deeper into slumber. Her mind now had relaxed and was about to dream. She even saw the smiling face of Akshay Kumar. Right then the whirring sound increased in decibels with every click, pierced her dream. She saw Akshay Kumar frowning and so was she.

'Damn!' She scrambled out of the bed. Why did her mother torture her like this in the morning? Only then did she realize that she wasn't home and it wasn't her mother using the mixer grinder. She was naked under the sheet. 'Naked? What did I do again?' She thought. She found her clothes were strewn on the floor and her floral bra precariously dangled from the corner of a chair. 'I will save you my soldier!' she muttered to the bra.

She quickly grabbed her bra and wore it. She felt a little less naked now. She raked her small hands through her long luscious black hair. Tied it, into a loose bun. She stood up and assessed herself in a stand-alone mirror stuck to a metal cupboard.

'Smoking hot!' She giggled, this story will be worth narrating to Ramya, her friend. She went to the bathroom in the room. She saw it was messy. A bucket overflowed with clothes and as she closed the doors, she saw his briefs hanging from the hook line.

'Ewww' she thought to herself. But her mind reminded her that she may have seen the parts hidden by these briefs last night. She rubbed the foggy mirror to clear it. She smoothed her hand over her face, feeling it soft and smooth. She splashed water from the tap and brushed her teeth with her finger. Who was he? How come she did not remember at all? Was she kidnapped? She laughed at that thought. She could not be kidnapped. No one would pay the ransom, at least not her father.

She picked up and wore the rest of her clothes. She looked around the room. The room had french windows on one side and blank walls on the other three sides. A queen-sized mattress lay on the floor. A table on the corner of the room with an ancient table lamp. A chair was adjacent to the table and her handbag was hooked on its arm.

She quickly checked her wallet. All her money was intact. She sighed. Then she remembered her phone, where was it? She went to the mattress, a cheap bedsheet covered it. She moved the pillows around and found her phone between the nook of the wall and the mattress. It had died, no battery charge was left. She looked at the table and found a charger hooked to the socket. She plugged her phone.

She tried to recollect what happened last night. She heard soft Hindi music playing outside the room. Ugh! She despised these tunes which played in an autorickshaw usually. The song lyrics were extremely romantic and played extra loud if the passenger was a female. To escape the sound she opened the French windows. She was pleasantly surprised to see a small balcony. Her mind suggested to find out in whose house she was in but she usually felt numb in the mornings. She strolled up to the edge of the balcony.

She looked down, she was on the first floor of a tall building. She saw a lady in an all-pink jumpsuit. Suddenly the lady waved at Kajal smiling. Kajal ducked behind. Oops! Who was that lady? She wondered. Should she have exposed herself like that? She didn't even know whose house she was at. She peeked from the edge again.

"Yoohoo. Hello. Good morning!" The lady screamed.

"Um. Good morning." Kajal gulped reluctantly.

"Are you Shrey's girlfriend?" The lady asked.

Shrey? So that's whose house she was at right now. Why is that name not ringing any bell for her? To answer the lady she just shook her head saying 'No'. That was safest. She had no idea what she was doing here? She thought she would have learned her lesson from last time. She shook her head in regret.

"Are you his friend?" The lady inquired.

'What a nosy bitch?' She thought to herself plastered a smile on her face. Let the peaceful morning spread some peace. Inside, that grinder and songs woke her up and now this lady was bothering her with a barrage of questions. She nodded her answer and waved at the lady. She retreated into the room.

She sat on the mattress, trying to recollect the events of last night. Alcohol and weed are the deadliest combinations for her. She should just stick to one next time or not at all. Vinod had the best weed, 'where did the bugger get it?' She wondered. He only got invited to parties for his stock. Maybe he was just a dealer. But she promised she would cut down on everything this year. Yet right after ten days from the vow, here she was sitting in a stranger's house, extremely relaxed and clueless about the night before. 'Kudos Kajal!' She patted her back.

Just then Shrey entered the room after a soft knock. 'Ah, manners!' She liked that and the rest that appeared after the knock. He was tall, lean and a head full of fabulous hair. Could anyone have such bright eyes and lips shaped like a bow? Nor was his skin fair nor was he dark, just the right shade. His Adam's apple bobbed nervously before he spoke to her.

"Hi, you are up?" What a voice, deep, deep baritone and sheepish smile as he pushed his hair back from his face. Kajal was assessing him as she met him for the first time.

"Hi." She said suggestively.

"Would you like some breakfast?" He asked.

Why couldn't she remember him at all? She smiled and her stomach grumbled in response.

"Uh, yes...let's have breakfast."

The rest of the house was barely furnished but the kitchen was equipped completely. She strolled the house trying to remember any fragment from last night. She looked outside the French windows while he set the plates out on a working counter of an open kitchen. Ah! An open kitchen is so modern and functional. As she looked out, she saw the pink jumpsuit lady pushing hard on the pedals of a stationary gym cycle in the garden. 'What a ghastly sight?' She thought.

She quickly turned towards some aromatic food. Her stomach grumbled in protest. He laughed. Why did he have to do that? The sound of his laughter had such a bass to it.

She smiled, "I hope you did not hear that?"

He happily said, "You will soon hear mine if we do not have breakfast." As an explanation, he said, "There is a banana melon smoothie, poha, toast, and even oats porridge." He offered her a plate of well-cut mixed fruits. "Here you can start with this."

"You made all of this?" She asked in amazement. He is a keeper. Maybe this wasn't a mistake. Ramya would say your fates have collided and you have found "The One".

"What one?" He asked.

'Oh no! Did I say that aloud?' She tried to focus on breakfast instead of his handsome face. 'I have to ask him, what shampoo he used?' She thought to herself.

"Umm I meant, I usually have just one thing for breakfast." She smirked.

"Oh! Feel free to try anything. Do you need eggs?" He said.

As if this spread wasn't enough, he tried to confuse her with another option of eggs. She spooned some poha on her plate and poured a glass of smoothie.

"Do you usually make such a grand breakfast?" She asked, eating from her plate.

"Is it too much?" He questioned guiltily, "I am practising to make different kinds of food."

"This is tasty, I usually do not have poha when made at home. But why are you trying different things?"

"Should I make something else?" He asked as he finished his plate of fruits.

"No, not at all. This is a lot."

They ate in silence. She thought she should ask him about last night.

"Listen about last night…" She purposely left the sentence hanging. She hoped he would complete it for her. He nodded as if she should continue. "I mean whatever happened…"

The doorbell rang distracting them from their conversation. He immediately opened it and Kajal had opened her mouth to eat toast. But she kept the toast aside and her mouth remained open. It was that lady in a pink jumpsuit.

"Ma, breakfast is ready. Come join us." He said.

'Oh no! Ma?' She thought. Her luck in these matters can be called 'Damn Unlucky'.

"Ahhh, later bunny, I came to meet your friend." She said and he looked confused. His mother explained, "I saw her on the balcony and we spoke."

"She is Rishab's friend. They had a party last night." He explained and both ladies looked at each other with renewed interest.

Now Rishab rang a bell in her memory. He was the one handing over all the smokes last night. He looked cute she thought last night but this guy in front of her was simply 'Hot stuff'.

"Where is Rishabh?" His mother asked the same question which Kajal wanted to ask.

"Ma don't you remember he was leaving today? He told me to tell you, sorry and tata." He laughed nervously. This exchange between them was interesting, Rishabh left. Right, he kept complaining about Mumbai at the party and everybody booed. Why couldn't she remember this guy from the party last night?

"He couldn't even say a proper goodbye to his aunt." Rishabh's aunty made a face and turned her attention to Kajal. She shivered slightly under his mother's scrutiny.

"Beta, I hope you had breakfast properly," Aunty asked kindly.

She nodded politely, "Yes, it's delicious."

His mother left them and instructed him to keep fresh coffee for her. He obediently poured coffee into the filter.

"So how do you know Rishabh?" She fished.

"Rishab is my cousin, he had an early morning flight. I think you must be sleeping."

'Yes Right.' She had no clue, how wasted was she? Damn girl!

"Listen Rishab told me to give you his number." He winked.

"I don't know what you are thinking…"

She started to say but he completed her sentence for her. "But I don't remember anything much from last night."

She looked stupidly at him and he laughed. "I know you were stoned last night. Rishab got you home to my surprise but apparently, you were the only one left and he could not get a coherent word from you."

Ah, that explains a lot but why was she naked? She couldn't even ask him what happened after Rishab got her home. This was extremely embarrassing.

"Thank you so much for having me and for the lovely breakfast." She was embarrassed.

"Don't be so formal. Relax, nothing happened."

"What do you mean?" her cheeks were burning red. There was an invisible smoke jetting out of her ears.

"We let you have the bedroom. Coffee?"

"No thanks, I should get going." She could not even face this handsome man anymore. She kept her eyes averted from him.

"Oh so soon? Here I thought we were just getting warmed up." He shook his head.

"I don't even know your name."

"My bad, I am Shrey by the way."

Finally, she looked up at him, his twinkling eyes below his messy hair, a bright white smile, and an extended hand. She shook it and felt a warmth spreading all over her body.

"I am a Kajal. The pleasure of meeting you is all mine." She smiled suggestively. Ramya would be so proud of her right, 'The One, Hot Stuff.'

6

Love At A Karaoke Bar

by Priyanka Sahi

I just love the feel of Goa, the cool sea breeze, the uber-cool atmosphere of the beaches, youngsters having fun on shacks, and not to forget the amazing food. It was 7 p.m. and my friends and I had just finished our water sports. Oh, what fun it was!

To introduce myself, I am Stella and I was in Goa for a friend's hen party. We were four girls and to say that, we were having the time of our lives is an understatement. Since it was our first time in Goa, we decided to do all the touristy stuff like visiting the beaches, heading to shacks for food and drinks, club-hopping, and whatnot.

On our second last day, we decided to visit a karaoke bar at one of the beaches. It was Friday night which meant it was buzzing with people - from locals to tourists, everyone seemed to have landed at the coolest place in India. I was on my third tequila shot of the day and the singer in me was shining brightly, I sang more songs than Lata Mangeshkar did in one film. Jokes apart, I was on a roll.

Another announcement was made with my name, I was sure the anchor knew my name by heart now. "We would request Ms Stella to join us on the stage for another song".

I heard my name and jumped on the stage in excitement. I was halfway through my song when I saw a familiar face in the crowd, it was a guy from my last office, seeing him in the crowd I lost my flow and abruptly ended my song. I thanked the audience for their kindness towards me and for bearing me with all my songs. I hurried towards my friends who were all badly drunk by now.

"Hey, I just saw the guy from my last office, the guy I had been crushing on since I joined that office", I told them all flustered from the booze and seeing my crush in the crowd.

"Oh really", my best friend replied, "what a coincidence, he's here at the very same time as you, why don't you go talk to him. It's a good opportunity, you know, since you couldn't gather the courage while he was in the same office. Maybe some booze and a push from your best friend may do the trick, go talk to him!!".

My friend said that as if it was so easy, maybe it's easy to say than doing it!

"Are you crazy, I spent two years ogling at him in the office, he must still think I'm some creep, and now you want me to go prove it to him? Thanks, but no thanks!", I huffed and let out a sigh.

Suddenly from the corner of my eye, I noticed a figure approaching our table, "Hey", the figure said shyly.

I could recognize this voice even from the farthest of places, it was this voice that kept me captivated in my last office for two years. I immediately looked toward him and gave out a nervous laugh.

"Sorry to disturb you like this but I know you from somewhere and I can't figure out where", he said scratching his head.

'Yup, I'm the creep who stared at you continuously in the office', I thought to myself rolling my eyes!

"Oh!" I started nervously, fidgeting with my hands, and sweating profusely. Could I be any weirder, I mentally slapped myself for being this nervous. "We kind of worked at the same office", I replied feeling shy. "I recognized you when I saw you in the crowd!"

"Yes! Right" he replied, now smiling and looking at me admiringly, "I think we were on the same floor; you look so different, I was thinking so hard as to where I had seen you. Great singing, by the way, I've become your fan." He said in a flirty way.

'Is the Rahul that I have been crushing on so hard for two years trying to flirt with me? Oh God, I must be dreaming!' I thought to myself.

"I'm Rahul, by the way", he said bringing out his hand for me to shake, I took no time to take his hand in mine and shook it till he started laughing. I immediately removed my hand from his after realizing I had held it for more than a minute.

"I'm here with a few of my friends from work, would you like to join me for a drink?" He asked.

I glanced at my friends who were already looking at me with a smirk, "Of course! Go ahead, we will be right here dancing and boozing, you go have fun with Rahul". They said his name in a teasing way, laying stress on every syllable and winking at me.

The night went by quickly, with me getting to meet Rahul's friends. My girls and I joined their group and made plans for the next two days in Goa. We visited a few more places and got to spend ample time together. Of course, Rahul and I exchanged numbers and stayed in touch after our meet-up in Goa.

After returning to Delhi, Rahul and I frequently exchanged messages on WhatsApp and met for lunches and dinners. Our offices were close by, so meeting him on weekdays was no problem. We usually went to karaoke bars as the newfound singer in me was now hyperactive. I never thought that Rahul and I would have so much in common. We both liked the same kind of songs, the same food, and more than anything I loved his sense of humour. It was so difficult to stay mad at him since he always had something funny to say.

We were at a coffee house discussing our childhood stories and fairy tales. "You know my favourite fairy-tale is the frog prince," I told him and he suddenly started croaking just like a frog. I almost choked up on my coffee as it was so funny.

He looked me in the eyes still croaking and said, "When does your frog get to become the prince?" He asked with a glint in his eyes. I blushed and looked away; I knew what he meant!

Rahul drove me back home. When we reached my house, he got down from the car and walked with me towards the door. Midway he started croaking again and I looked at him laughing. I could now control my feelings anymore and I jumped on him and kissed him.

"You are my forever frog prince, you idiot, I love you so much," I said and hid my face at the crook of his neck.

"I love you, too, my wicked queen." He said that laughing and I slapped his arm.

"You're so mean," I said still hugging him.

"Yeah I know but I'm also a gentleman because I have been holding a hundred kgs in my arms for almost two minutes now but did I complain? Nope, not at all." He said laughing. That statement earned him a few more slaps on his arms.

"You're so annoying; I don't know how I fell for you?" I said.

"Well, my froggy croak is pretty alluring." He said laughing.

"Can you ever be serious?" I asked laughing.

"If I was serious I would be in the hospital no, my lady?" He said winking at me.

"Oh! You and your never-ending jokes. Start doing stand-up comedy, you'll earn more." I said laughing.

"Oh no! I don't want my jokes to become public, these are exclusively for you." He said smiling. With that, he dropped me on the floor. I fell with a thud and glared at him.

"Why did you drop me, you could have asked me to get off."

"Oh, what fun would that be." He said and ran away.

I ran after him and as soon as I caught hold of him, I started slapping his arms, "I hate you; I hate you, you're so mean Rahul." I said still glaring at him, he looked at me and came closer, I could feel his breath on my face and I knew I was getting redder every passing second.

"I know!" with that, he ran away again and I was left dumbfounded.

'I don't know how I fell for this doofus?' I said smiling at the thought.

Today when I see the diamond ring on my finger, I feel so glad that I drank all that alcohol in the karaoke bar in Goa. It brought out the singer in me. Otherwise, I would have never met the love of my life, Rahul.

7

Wink And Miss

by Vishakha Naware

It was a cold winter morning and Ananth had woken up early groggily for an important meeting. He grunted and was seriously irritated, but he had no option as it was a new job in a new country. He reached the office just in time for the Besprechung or the meeting and was not focused on what was happening around him. The only thing he could think of was his warm and cosy bed and his fleece blanket. He wanted to curl up in that and not attend some meetings discussing profits and losses and sales pitches.

"Okay, die Besprechung ist zu Ende. Wir treffen uns später. Auf Wiedersehen," said Herr (Mr.) Hofmann. Ananth was suddenly woken up from his daydreaming antics and he just stared at Hofmann. Everyone started to leave but Ananth's gaze was fixed at Hofmann.

Hofmann was puzzled and said to Ananth, "Herr Rajan, das Meeting ist zu Ende!". He said every word slowly and carefully as if talking to a child. When that didn't work, he then gestured that the meeting is over and that Ananth could leave.

Ananth's face went red with embarrassment. How could he not understand 'Ende' when it's so close to English. His mind wandered to his German classes. He was a brilliant student, a topper in everything except Deutsch. Deutsch was a pet peeve, his Achilles heel.

He was transported back to the classroom with modern tables and chairs and modern methods of teaching back in India. 'We teach interactively'; the teacher had said on the first day of class. He liked the classes but not the language so much and especially not the grammar! He especially had difficulty with the articles. 'Why was a lamp feminine but a book neutral and a pen masculine?' He used to wonder. He found no logic to it at all! He would stare at objects and try and imagine their genders, he would put post-its on them to remember, but he just couldn't! The same happened with cases- Akkusativ and Dativ. Such fancy names! The verbs used to dance in his head. The verb 'helfen' which means to help, would speak to him and say, 'I need Dativ' and would take the Dativ article.

'Oh my God!' Ananth used to say pounding his head when he tried to solve the exercises. The grammatical jargon would all mix up in his head.

His mind came back to reality and he realized that it was his fourth day in office in Stuttgart and most of the meetings happened in German. He had certificates to prove that he was fluent in German. But that was just theory. In practice, it was very difficult for him to understand the language, the accent, and the pace. Speaking it was a different ballgame altogether! He would stutter and somehow manage to speak a few sentences.

He remembered an incident. He had just landed in Stuttgart and had taken a taxi to go to his apartment. The taxi driver smiled at him and asked him, "Guten Tag! Wohin?" (Good day, where to).

Ananth had screamed, "Akkusativ!" The German taxi driver couldn't stop laughing the whole journey.

Ananth's boss, Mr Hofmann was a chilled-out guy and a great boss. He would explain many things to Ananth. So would his colleagues. He had heard the stereotype that the Germans are cold and unfriendly people. But it was so damn untrue! They were very understanding and accommodating of him. Of course, they spoke fluent English but most of the activities took place in German and they would guide Ananth regularly. He was slowly getting used to the language and gaining some confidence in speaking. He could carry out basic conversations at the store or on public transport.

It was a boring long day at work. He glanced at his watch clock and it was 5.00 pm, time to leave. The Germans took the office hours very seriously. Work was work and private life was private. They never mixed both of them. The boss and the colleagues were supposed to meet later at a bar to celebrate a birthday.

"We will meet at 7.30 pm opposite Lidl. You know, the supermarket." Hofmann said to Ananth using all the gestures he could, waving his hands frantically in the air.

Ananth looked at him transfixed and with slight amusement.

"Und dann, wenn Sie mich sehen, winken Sie! Okay. See you then," said Hofmann to Ananth and left.

Ananth was very puzzled. 'When you see me, wink at me. Did I understand him correctly? I mean it was nice of him to offer to wait for me and take me to the bar as I'm new here. But this is a strange request.' He thought aloud. Then he wondered, maybe this is acceptable in the German culture and dismissed the whole thing.

He went home quickly and changed into some casuals. As this was a private event, he had to wear casual clothing. He was very lucky that within just a few days of joining the office, he was invited to such an intimate office event. It was a rarity and he didn't want to miss the opportunity. He believed he looked dapper in the white T-shirt and Levi's jeans that he was wearing. He took the S-Bahn and reached the street where Lidl was located. He, of course, had a GPS on his phone and could easily locate the bar but he didn't want to come out as a prude to his boss since the boss had so generously offered to wait for him.

He reached Lidl and waited for a few minutes. There were still five more minutes till their meeting time. The Germans took time and punctuality very seriously, even at casual events. This was a stark contrast to India, where coming fashionably late at casual events was the 'in' thing.

At exactly 7 pm, the meeting time, he saw his boss standing opposite the supermarket. As requested, he started winking at his boss. Hofmann didn't see him initially, but after a few minutes, he saw Ananth winking at him. He looked puzzled and amused at the same time. He gestured for him to cross the road and come to his side. So Ananth crossed the road. Thankfully, now he had to stop winking. Hofmann was looking at him full of intrigue.

Hofmann looked at him for a moment and broke into a laugh. "Was machen Sie? What are you doing? Why were you winking at me? That's strange. Is it an Indian thing?"

Colour drained from Ananth's face as he realized that he might have goofed up something. "No, it's not an Indian thing. I thought it's a German thing. You told me- Wenn Sie mich sehen, winken Sie. When you see me, wink at me!" Ananth explained, trying to avoid looking at Hofmann directly.

Now Hofmann just burst into laughter and tears started rolling out of his eyes. "Ach du liebe Zeit! Oh my god, winken doesn't mean winking, it means to wave. I told you to wave at me when you see me. You misunderstood!"

Ananth was amused and embarrassed at his faux pas.

"Come on! What a great story and an intercultural lesson to give to the others." Hofmann looked at Ananth and gestured him to join him. Ananth knew that he was going to be the talk of the office for quite some time now.

Who said Germans have no sense of humour? He looked at his boss and smiled.

8

Aliens

by Susan Bowman

It happened, just as the clock struck midnight!

It had been a wonderful evening; my granddaughter was home from university and we had gone out for dinner. At her suggestion, we'd eaten at one of those trendy burger restaurants favoured by the young and I have to say, the entire experience was surprising. The food was superb and the atmosphere electric. I enjoy having Sarah stay, she's a breath of fresh air, always teaching me new things on my laptop as if the adult child roles had reversed. She never patronized but could occasionally be seen rolling her eyes if I made what seemed to her to be a ridiculous suggestion or when I failed to understand instruction.

"Oh, Nana!" She'd say, "you're so funny."

She meant I was naive or behind the times. I'd be tempted to remind her that I taught her to eat with a knife and fork, write her name, and use the bathroom. I smile and remark that we can't all be as smart as her.

That night was bitterly cold, frosty, the sky was clear and full of stars. We stood huddled together on the drive admiring them before gratefully re-entering the warmth of my little cottage. I live on the very edge of Donneton, a pretty village that bursts with life in the summer and hibernates when the winter months close in. My family worries about my isolation, can't comprehend why I'm happy here and send relatives to check on me. They think I don't know what's going on but I'm old - not senile.

Putting a log on the fire, we settled down to watch a late-night movie on the television, it was a classic Sarah said, had them screaming in the aisles in the 70's she said. How we giggled at its poor attempts to frighten us with poltergeists and crazy people who sought out the supernatural. Not at all scary yet, I did jump once or twice.

I was closing the curtains before making my way upstairs to bed when I saw it. I was admiring the icy patterns left on the windowpane, trying to remember an old rhyme about Jack Frost. A lighted globe was travelling over the blackened sky. Radiant and silent it crossed a path between the trees, rising slowly and smoothly from my right to my left. It was large in a vast sky, not perfectly round but spherical, no, egg-shaped. At first bright enough to make me shield my eyes, the light gradually faded as it passed.

I stood watching incredulously, I'm sure my jaw dropped open. What was this? Then, before I had time to question, and just as it disappeared from view, another appeared, slightly brighter and higher still.

"Sarah, quickly, come and look at this. You won't believe it." I shouted to my granddaughter, who was in the kitchen making cocoa. As I watched the second orb trace a path over the trees the possibilities hit me. I grabbed the windowsill to steady myself, a mixture of fear and excitement washed over me. I wasn't sure why but my nerves were building, I trembled a little, my mouth was dry, I shuddered, yet I was unable to look away. I suppose it was partly due to the stillness of the trees, eerily white tipped in the starlight, partly to do with that ridiculous film, but I have to admit me feeling quite uneasy.

"Sarah," I called again, "I need you, oh gosh, come and look at this." Even I could hear the concern in my voice. Was I overreacting to what I was seeing? What was I seeing?

"Yes, I saw them through the kitchen window, Nana, let's go outdoors for a proper look." Sarah seemed unperturbed. Had she seen them before I wondered, perhaps she knew what they were; she was after all studying physics at uni? She wasn't at all worried about the strange apparition; confidence was her middle name. I mused as we shrugged into coats. Somehow her self-assurance fed my discomfort. Why didn't she see the potential apocalypse that I foresaw, the catastrophe that this sighting predicted? She was decidedly blasé about the lights in the sky, for goodness sake she appeared happy to see them as if it were a positive experience!

In slippered feet, we made our way outside and pressed together, her against the cold, me for support. There were some comfort and a little warmth in her embrace but Sarah was a small girl and I wondered how much protection she could offer if... There we stood that night on the little square of lawn that fronted my tiny home and watched the procession of brightly lit UFOs as they passed our piece of heaven.

"So pretty. Don't you think Nana?"

Three, four, five, seven in all and yes, they were pretty but so were deadly flowers, viruses under a microscope, poisonous snakes and I wasn't being fooled. I was as they say, gobsmacked. Silenced by the splendour of these things, by the cold, by fright. I'm seventy-eight years old and I've seen some things nobody should have to witness, things to make your toes curl, turn your stomach over, I've seen things I wish I could un-see but that night was special. I can honestly say the combination of dread and excitement was spectacular, not knowing whether to worry or celebrate - breath-taking.

"Aren't they beautiful nana?" Gushed Sarah as she gave me an extra tight squeeze.

"Beautiful?" I challenged her, "aren't you concerned that we're being invaded?"

Sarah giggled. "Oh Nana," she laughed, "those aren't aliens, they're Chinese lanterns!"

Sarah explained that the menacing shapes were only made of paper with extremely lightweight frames, they had little platforms inside on which was cradled a tea light. As the candle burned it warmed up the air within allowing the lantern to rise, the breeze carried it along.

"I can imagine how confused you were Nana, if you haven't seen them before, they're quite spooky aren't they?" Sarah conceded, "The fuel source in each sky lantern burns for about eight-ten minutes, which is how they travelled out of sight and they can reach heights of over a thousand feet." She added, "and they can travel up to three miles away from where they were lit."

I smiled wryly, "I'm so dumb, I thought they were alien spaceships. How stupid am I?" I said. "You know, the funny thing is I was kind of excited about meeting Martians."

Sarah took my cold hand, raised it to her equally chilled lips, and kissed it. "Come on Nana, let's get our cocoa and go to bed. I think we've had enough excitement for one night."

"I wonder where they came from, we're so far from anyone."

"I don't know Nana, somebody's having a party in the village?"

As I was pulling the blind down in my bedroom a little later, something caught my eye. It was a long way off so I couldn't be sure but...

I didn't say anything about my bonus sighting to Sarah in the morning. We sat together over breakfast laughing about what had happened and I did cringe with embarrassment although she assured me that mistaking Chinese lanterns for alien spaceships was a common mistake but I could tell she was disappointed in my naivety.

"Oh look, Nana, you're not alone in thinking alien invasion last night," said Sarah waving her mobile phone at me, "there are fourteen posts in the neighbourhood group describing the UFOs. Oh my," she explained, "this one saw little green men!"

"Well," I replied, "thank goodness I'm not the only fool in the village" I laughed.

Sarah drained her coffee cup and gathering together her bits and pieces she hugged me goodbye. She placed her bags in the boot of the car, and waving goodbye she shouted back, "You know what's odd Nana? Not one post on the village website mentioned a party or gathering that might have set off those lanterns. Where they came from is quite a mystery."

I made myself a cup of tea and settled down to watch the local midday news. Towards the end of the bulletin, at the point where humorous items are usually aired, the presenter began talking about several UFO sightings that had occurred over the last twenty-four hours.

"At first these observations were dismissed as Chinese lanterns but because of the number reported and the area covered – "he trailed off. I smiled smugly. I wondered, I just wondered...

9

I'll Always Be There For You

by Shaikh Abdul Wasee

The bell hanging at the cafe door rang and they both hugged each other and sat down.

"It's been a long time, buddy. Twelve years."

Prakash took a sip of coffee, chuckled, and said, "Yes, Twelve years."

"Where are Bhupendra and Sweetie?"

"On the way. How are you?"

"I am great. What about you? Got married or a girlfriend?"

"Naah! I am better off as a single person. Love is just not for me."

"Still got that tag on your name? Prince Prajapati?"

Snehal laughed mimicking his fake accent and Prakash a.k.a Prince giggled with her and replied, "That was so silly dude but I am better with Prakash now. Simple name, simple way of life."

"Still got your scooter that would need a kick to start?" Snehal smiled at this question and imitated Prakash's action of driving a scooter to which he got annoyed.

"If not for that scooter, you guys wouldn't have got to travel around Dehradun, huh! You should thank me."

"Still the angry young guy, huh?"

Prakash and Snehal both shared a laugh and sipped some coffee.

"Are they both coming?"

"I don't know. They got the mail but didn't answer."

Prakash ordered some chips and continued with coffee. Snehal talked in a bit of a low tone and said, "It shouldn't have happened."

"Snehal it wasn't in our control. Nobody's to blame here. It was just bad luck."

"Yes, bad luck which cost both their lives in a way no one can imagine."

"Even I can't forget that day. Bhupendra was so happy. He glowed differently with her; you know. In twelve years of school life, he always kept talking about grades and placements but when she arrived in our lives, he was so... different. He actually lived."

"Remember the first day of the coaching classes of you guys? You both were on your scooter and got late for the test."

Prakash chuckled at this point and grabbed a chip and put it in his mouth making a crunchy sound to which Snehal hit him on his shoulder and they both laughed.

"How can I forget that day man. We both got late for the test and the professor could see our mouths full of the peanuts, that Bhupendra and I were eating on our way to the institute.

Before the lecture started, we got a ten-minute lecture on the importance of time."

"There used to be his favourite quote, some one-liner or something, right?"

"I will say, *Bachcha (Child)! Time and tide wait for none.*"

"And you being an idiot, asked in response, *Sir, who is none?*"

Snehal and Prakash both laughed on this one and ordered some more chips and coffee. Sipping the coffee, Prakash continued. "Those were the days, dude. No stress, no constant need for money. Just our small world. I still remember when Bhupendra saw Sweetie for the first time. He was staring at her as if she was some playdate video. And in reality, she did was got in the wrong class thinking it is of algebra which was chemistry. But pun intended, Sweetie made a variable change in Bhupendra and he got a new set of chemicals flowing in his brain."

"Do you remember the chemistry practical incident of his?"

"I can still visualize his spoilt shirt every time I remember it."

Snehal and Prakash laugh so hard that they did not realize that the whole cafeteria was staring at them. Then they got quiet but still chuckled. Prakash said, "It was those stupid chemistry practicals and he was holding test tube with a holder and Sweetie just saw him from the outside of the lab and smiled at her as an acquaintance does and this idiot waved at her with the hand, he was holding the liquid. The whole liquid splashed on his lab coat and his white shirt. It was as if he spilt curry on his shirt. It was so funny for us but embarrassing for him to walk around like that but everything changed during the questionnaire when something amazing happened. Sweetie and Bhupendra had their questionnaire at the same time in the same class. They both were sitting next to each other. And my idiot friend was dumbstruck and dead silent after seeing her. Our professor was shocked to see Bhupendra with no answers and Sweetie answered her questions with ease and also gave a look to Bhupendra for concentrating on the questions. As soon as Sweetie went Bhupendra came to his senses and he answered all questions."

Snehal laughed and replied, "Bhupendra was so in love, man. Remember the time when we four went for a lunch break and he was refusing?"

"Yea, I do. He was giving the reasons for his test and studies and as soon as Sweetie caught with us for the lunch, he agreed and smiled. Silly guy, he was."

Snehal chuckled and added, "Yes, the silly guy who helped you pass the tests."

"Yes, he did. Remember the annual day dance?"

"Yes, I do. Can't forget that. I was paired with you. But luckily Sweetie was paired with Bhupendra. He used to smile a lot while dancing with her. They also went for a walk after the annual day. They were the real people feeling the dance and the music."

"It rained after the occasion too. And that turned out to be the worst days of our lives. I still remember rushing down to the hospital with you. Looking at her in that condition, still makes me sick revisiting those memories."

"Still don't know what would have happened after that when Bhupendra didn't come to see her even once."

Snehal and Prakash both sipped coffee while a car arrived outside the cafeteria. A man in suits and trousers picked up a lady from the car and helped her sit on the wheelchair and adjusted it to her convenience. They both entered the cafe. Prakash and Snehal smiled at the scene and they saw the man and lady approaching them.

The couple smiled and said, "Don't you guys remember the weird couple from the annual day dance?"

Snehal and Prakash both hugged them as they recognized they were Sweetie and Bhupendra. And all of them sat down and started to discuss the old memories as Prakash questioned about the annual day, Bhupendra excused himself for the reason of ordering something for him and walked towards the counter. Sweetie understood his nervousness and said, "He never abandoned me. When you guys came to meet me, he was scared of my parents so he just stood far away. Then when you guys entered the corridor, he ran and hid in the toilet. He came out and met my parents after you guys left. After that incident, he confessed his love to me and told my parents that he wanted to marry me. My parents didn't say yes immediately, and even Bhupendra told them to take their time. My parents started making calls looking for another alliance to marry me but nobody wanted to marry a bald girl in a wheelchair. My parents didn't like Bhupendra but that didn't stop him from coming every day to the hospital to check if I am okay. He kept a record of my menstrual cycle. He even stayed with my parents just to see if they would be okay handling the stress. My parents permitted me to marry him by not just being fed up with his love for me, but because he never gave up on me, even when I was hurt and different from other girls. Before that accident, we both were drenched in rain and I had told him that love is nothing but just your mind playing games with you temporarily. When he heard me say that, I saw his face and I knew he was broken. We both started walking again and all of a sudden, a bus slipped through and my body smashed its sidewalls. I thought Bhupendra got lucky getting away with it. But he was in pain worse than mine. The pain of losing me. Again. But he still didn't give up on me."

Bhupendra arrived with the coffee and questioned Snehal about her tears, "Why are you crying?"

"Nothing, just some dust."

Sweetie grabbed the coffee, sipped, and said "It's not because of you okay. You are so much in love with yourself that you think everyone will cry for you when you arrive, huh? She was crying for me because I am her best friend."

Sweetie winked at Snehal and smacked her hair towards Bhupendra. Everybody laughed and sipped the coffee. Prakash grabbed a chip and made the crunchy sound of biting it and the rest of the three looked at him with an irritated face and yelled at him in unison, "Prince stop it, you idiot."

Everybody laughed and the conversational stories continued.

10

Moment In Space

by Vaishali Chandorkar Chitale

Raghu sat back in his chair and smiled at Ananya, his wife. Catching his glance, she smiled back enquiringly. They were having their evening downers and sat in companionable silence. He was in a mellow mood and loved this part of the day the most. Sitting with his wife of thirty-eight years, after a hard day's work, this for him was nirvana; he was at peace with himself and his surroundings.

He and Ananya had married when arranged marriages were the norm and marrying for love were far off the horizon. It was after all the decade of the early eighties when the young couples of his generation did not dare to face their parents to talk about girls and choices; parents, as their parents before them were averse to change the ongoing tradition of finding the 'right' bride for their son (and so for the family) and saw it as their prerogative! The outdated thinking that she isn't just marrying the man of the house, but also his family still prevailed in most homes. So many like him, the true-blue obedient sons, could never think of rocking the boat and went with the flow.

Seeing her looking at him again with a question in her eyes, he asked her whether she remembered their first meeting. She smiled at that memory and asked him teasingly, "Are the bells still chiming?"

"Oh, yes, absolutely!" he replied with a laugh. "Do you again want to hear what I had told your brother so many years ago when he was in a quandary about finding a girl of his choice? What happened when we first met?" he asked her. "And how did I know 'you' are the one?"

"Yes, please!", she replied, her eyes shining, happy to hear again, as usual, how his heart had skipped a beat on seeing her some thirty-odd years ago and it still did!

Laughing at her delight, he launched into his story.

"Ding-dong, ding-dong… the bells will chime in your heart", he remembered, telling his BIL (Brother-in-law, for those who came in late) when he had asked him about how to know that SHE is the one!" Is that what happened with you when you saw my sister?", this small innocuous question from his BIL, took him back to the time when he had first laid his eyes on his wife-to-be!

He had told his BIL to persevere and be patient, as he had been. He had himself done the mandatory rounds of 'seeing' the girls, found to be 'appropriate' by his parents, and nothing had done the trick. The tense silence at home always had said it all. Again, he had failed to please his parents with his rejection of the latest girl paraded in front of him to lure him to tie the knot. To hear his mother say it, one would have felt that he had committed the biggest crime ever, instead of just saying no to a girl; who incidentally did not make him weak-kneed with joy or made him want to dance with gay abandon. How does one explain to a parent the all-important aspect of liking a girl? You know - she's the one – when the bells start ringing, when the world appears sharper and brighter in all its vibrant colours; when you have a goofy smile on your face, even while doing brain-killing number-crunching work in the office?

The X-factor that he had been looking for, trying to explain it is as difficult as nailing jelly to a tree, was just not there. What was this elusive 'X' factor? He guessed it's different strokes for different folks! For him it was on closing his eyes if he could visualise lots of laughter and joy in each other's company and both of them sitting in compatible silence thirty-odd years hence, THAT was it!! She had to press all the right buttons for it to work, and he was ready to wait a lifetime to find his soul mate; notwithstanding his parents' pressure to marry. They in their wisdom thought that life was passing him by and soon 'no eligible' girls would be left for him as all the good ones would have been snapped up if he doesn't hurry with his choice. Undeterred he had turned a blind eye to their cajoling looks every time he went home on leave.

"Life has a way of jolting you of your stupor when you least expect it," he exclaimed to his BIL who was riveted by his story. Here he was happily cruising through life as a seagull floating on ocean waters, ignoring his parents' beseeching looks when they asked him to 'see' yet another girl as a favour to them. They could not refuse the acquaintance who had brought the proposal and so there they had trooped again, en masse as a family for yet another chai-and-poha session and a hopeful look in his parents' eyes.

He still remembered the faintly bored stance of his and 'oh-no- not- again' look on his face receiving the first hard kick on his abdomen on seeing the 'girl' for the first time, and he had jack-knifed to sit straight and look presentable. An amused smile on his mother's face had told him that she had noted his reaction and had smiled to herself. His BIL laughed with amusement as he too had seen his reaction when Ananya had first walked into the room.

Whoosh! had gone his heart, and suddenly, he had found himself wanting to make a right 'impression'. When they went to sit a little further away from the families, he had been was enthralled by her talk which his dazed senses actually hadn't registered, he now admitted sheepishly. The hours just flew by!! Before he had known it, it had been 9.30 pm and a gentle nudge from his mother had made him aware that the family was waiting politely for both of them to join everyone so that they could bid goodbyes.

He hadn't wanted the evening to end. At home, he had pestered his parents by talking incessantly about her and they had exchanged amused looks between them. He had made them sit and talked about her till late in the night, and his poor exhausted parents had indulged him, no doubt relieved that finally their ordeal of finding a 'suitable girl' was over and done with.

Present Day…

Recalling with a smile he told Ananya now that his BIL had looked at him with deep admiration then. "When your family had deterred and wanted some more time," he recalled telling his BIL, "I had made a beeline the very next day to your place to assuage any doubts your parents had of my career and prospects and our life together."

He was happy that Rahul (his BIL) and Shweta had thirty-five years of wedded bliss behind them and it made him a wee bit happy that he had played a small part in their story. His musings had reverberated with his brother-in-law and he too had found his soul mate.

What was it about Ananya, he thought now that had him so sure that she was THE one? Yes, she was (and still is) attractive, bright, and intelligent but it was her joie-de-vivre as opposed to his reticent nature, her bubbly self and vivaciousness, her charm and confidence that was not deterred by his imposing silence that had made his heart beating faster than a greyhound in a race. So enthralled had he been by her that he had harassed his mother-quite unlike him - to give his in-laws an assertive answer as soon as they could.

He had literally bulldozed Ananya's parents into agreeing, he now recalled with a laugh. Ananya playfully punched him in the arm, thanking her stars for his persistence. Thirty-eight years of a roller coaster ride, with more ups than downs and he would not have it any other way. They had shared years of laughter, some inevitable tears but they had weathered it together.

Now at the cusp of their silver years, with their children charting out their own path, they were free to live for themselves and sit back and reflect on the 'road not taken', and happily living their remaining years with contented smiles.

Oh yes, and in case you're wondering, the bells are still chiming merrily away!

11

Not Knowing When To Let Go

by Anita Gonsalves

Rahul a three-year-old boy was the only son of his parents. He had been pampered by his grandparents who took care of him while both his parents were working. However, his parents were very strict but loving and ensured that once they came back from work, the entire time was devoted to Rahul. Hence Rahul turned out to be a well-mannered, observant, reserved, and shy boy. He had been taught good values & most importantly never to raise his hand or hit anyone.

Rahul began attending kindergarten school. However, because of his shy and reserved nature, he was very slow in making friends.

Kalp another boy in his class on the other hand was the opposite. He was a very mischievous kid. He loved bullying kids in his class however he had no such luck with other kids as they were always in groups and this frightened him.

Once during lunch break, he noticed Rahul sitting all alone having his food. He kept observing Rahul for a few days and realized Rahul was more of a quiet person having no friends and the ideal target for him.

The next day, Kalp went near Rahul during lunch break and said hi to him. Rahul as usual did not respond and was busy eating as he was aware of Kalp's bullish behaviour. This angered Kalp and he punched Rahul on his back saying, "I said hi you dumbo!"

Rahul was too stunned to react however he just moved from there and went and sat near the door of the classroom.

Kalp was angry and confused at the same time wondering what Rahul was doing near the door and went back to his seat. The lunch break ended and the teacher entered the class. Rahul complained to the teacher however when confronted Kalp refused his act and insisted he was innocent and that he was just playing with Rahul.

The teacher believed Kalp and told Rahul there must be some mistake and that they could continue playing safe without getting her involved.

Rahul was too stunned and not knowing what to say decided to keep quiet.

The next day during lunch break, Kalp had his chance again and he punched Rahul on his back and ran away. Rahul knowing that the teacher would not believe him and as he was taught never to raise his hand, felt frustrated but decided to let go again.

This happened for the entire week, with Kalp's punches getting bolder and harder. The devilish laugh on Kalp's face made Rahul cringe with pain & fright. He then decided to inform his dad.

Once when eating his dinner, Rahul informed his dad about Kalp and his punches. His dad asked him, "Why didn't you tell the teacher and insist that he was troubling you."

"I could not as this happened in her absence and Kalp could make her believe him."

Unable to see his kid sad, Rahul's dad whispered in his ear, "I have a trick. Here it goes."

The next day, Rahul with confidence albeit with a little hesitation waited for the lunch break. The minute he felt Kalp was near him, he stood guard. As soon as, Kalp raised his hand to punch Rahul, Rahul immediately swung back and caught Kalp's hand twisting it.

"Let me go. What are you doing?" Kalp cried.

"I am just doing what I had to do a long time back," Rahul replied.

"Let me go I said, you will have to pay for this."

"We will see."

"Come on Rahul, you are hurting me. Let me go."

Rahul did not leave Kalp's hand. Kalp was crying in pain due to the firm grip of Rahul's hand. The entire class was staring at the duo. The break was over in a few minutes. The teacher entered the class and was shocked at the sight before her eyes. She immediately asked Rahul to release his hand and called for his parents.

Rahul's dad entered the class confused at what had happened. The teacher then showed him the marks on Kalp's hand.

"I am very sorry to inform you that your kid needs certain disciplinary action for what he has done. This is just not acceptable." The teacher said in an annoyed tone.

"Rahul, please come here and explain this. Why did you hold Kalp's hand twisting it and not letting go?" Rahul's dad asked Rahul.

"Dad he is the same boy who punches me every day. The teacher did not believe me hence I had told you about this."

Rahul turned to the teacher and said, "My parents have taught me never to raise my hand on anyone and hence I did not hit back Kalp when he punched me first and informed you. But you did not believe me neither did the other classmates come to my defence. I let it go. But this made Kalp bolder and he started hitting me every day. Hence I informed my dad who shared the trick."

"What trick?" The teacher questioned.

Rahul's dad then recalled his conversation with his son and was still unable to fathom what exactly happened.

"When Kalp came to hit me today, I caught his hand twisting it thereby not allowing him to hit me back."

"But why did you not let go of his hand when he started crying in pain."

Rahul looking at his dad said, "Because my dad gave me this trick however he did not tell me what to do next and hence I kept holding his hand."

Poor Rahul had tears in his eyes wondering where did he go wrong. Rahul's dad too embarrassed to speak and not knowing how to explain himself just kept looking at his feet. He only meant to teach the child self-defence.

While the teacher had a good laugh at the child's innocence but felt sad at the other child being hurt.

Kalp on the other hand was amused and angry at the same time. He nevertheless apologized, took his bag, and ran out of the classroom vowing never to cross paths again with Rahul, thereby learning his lesson.

12

Once Upon In An Indian Marriage

by Arundhati Sahoo

Here I was, at yet another wedding function. So, my neighbour was getting married and I thought why not go and attend the function, in the meantime treat my tongue to a good feast for free. So, I searched my wardrobe for a flashy saree and decided to put it on. After all, marriages are all about flashing and flaring. I put on a cherry red saree with stonework and embroidery on the borders that my madam gave me, it was an old one, she said. But I don't get the old and new of rich people, she would say this is old and happily flash around torn pants for fashion. Anyway, who understands these rich people, they put photos of eating salad and instead eat the fried rice and oily curries in reality with so much sumptuousness.

I never understand them, so I rather came back to my world, after all, got this chance to flaring myself after a long time, so I put on a jhumka, a typical Indian earring designed only for such occasions as I believe, otherwise who would wear something to work that makes a sound with each step you take. I mean it's not like the sound of high pointed heels that make the tok tok tok like in those web series, my madam watches. She also tries to wear these small skirts; I think she buys them a smaller size or something and flaunts it like it's fashion. I have never been there or done that but I just know because I have seen a lot of that world, thanks to my job.

So, yeah, coming to the marriage, I went all spiced up and with all my glamour to find the other neighbour aunty Mrs. Das just near the entry. I got a good opportunity to enter in a pair rather than being single. Oh, Mr Das, you must be thinking, well, he was out in the Men's zone smoking a cigarette and having some fun time along with the worse half of mine. So, I and Mrs. Das entered into the function. I in red and she is in a maroon colour saree with a waistband and armlets and of course the jhumka.

We went to the bride's room so that we could hand over our parcels. Well, everybody in the neighbourhood brings parcels as wedding gifts, but this time I had decided to give a gift. I have had this tea set kept with me for the last three years. I got it as a gift at my wedding, why not use that instead? So, I gifted her that and Mrs. Das gave an envelope to her.

The point is not about our gifts but Mrs. Sharma's. She lives just down the lane with her son and daughter-in-law. All three of them were there at the wedding. While giving the parcel to the bride, her parcel slipped through her hands and fell. The thing that stirred quite the discussion is that nothing came out of the parcel. She must have purposefully kept it empty and came here for a free feast with the family.

Now, this did upset Mrs. Das quite a bit. She went on to say, "Look, that's quite a brain. I mean, if you could just manage to hand over the parcel without dropping it, this game would be interesting. We could dine for free and go home. Anyway, gifts are just a waste of money."

I was slightly in agreement with her and just nodded. I mean, even if it's a three-year-old gift yet it's a good one and we need to be cautious of society at least. What people would say! I can't stand there like Mrs. Sharma. I had come here from Bangalore. Now, people do look at us with some respect, don't they? I can have the sambhar rice there but back here in Durgapur, I need to have my fish and that too in style.

Bangalore is after all a metro city that I have come from and it all means status for me. It's really difficult to manage the perception here in small cities, people look at everything you do. It's not like there, where people don't see, they are too busy to notice anything you know. But they do point out the specks of dust that remain once I clean, but not like this. My husband cooks there for five houses and I do the cleaning. Because of the pandemic, we both have come back to the village as the people there shifted back to their hometown. But, here, I have told everyone that we have a hotel in Bangalore and my husband was the chef. After all, I have to keep up the status. I told them that I am the manager of our hotel and I take care of the waiters, who take orders and clean utensils etc. We also eat the hotel food daily, I mean, the status I have to keep.

I could see Mr Das entering into the hall and what I couldn't believe was on one side of him was my dear irritating consort, whom I have been bonded with for seven lives yet it's difficult to bear him for seven days. On the other side of Mr Das, there was my ex-boyfriend, with whom I spent good seven years roaming around in his rickshaw. Quite a scene you would think, but for me, my legs started trembling, and yet my stomach was all about the ruffling of butterflies now.

I just wished Mrs. Das would ask that we go somewhere else. But she couldn't control her excitement so I instead looked forward to patching up with Mrs. Sharma. But my Mr Worst half called me from behind and I couldn't but hear him.

I asked him, "Where have you been my love, I was waiting; I thought you forgot."

He looked at me, happily amazed and so did my ex-boyfriend. But on his face, it was not happiness but astonishment. I escaped from there with my husband and we went for dinner. Now, this is the time I had been waiting for. I went there, had a sumptuous meal. The juice was a little watery and the fish was not local, I could just tell it from the smell. It's not that I am boasting or anything, but I used to also sell fishes and from there I know. It doesn't always need you to have been there and done that but well, sometimes all you have to do is be an Indian to know it all even without knowing it.

So, I indeed paid my regards with the comments on the feast and prepared to leave as fast as possible. My Mr Worst half was however in a mood to have romance and all, of course, he took the early escape as a hint. But who would again make the Indian men understand the difference between a hint and anything other than a hint from a girl. Especially when it's the wife; they are a breed who don't even understand the difference between lipstick and lip gloss.

So, I was now left with two options, either to succumb to this man's voluptuous needs or to be the lady that I was. I entered the house and told him to wait as I wanted to freshen up. I straight away went to the washroom to clean up my makeup and in the process, I brought my real face to come forward. When I came out of the washroom, he looked at me with a scrunched nose as if he smelled some stinky gas. But it was actually me, who smelled that; Yes; he had released that, 'maybe the food from the feast' he said, but that just turned me off.

He continued to make a face at me and kind of shut me down. It seems I couldn't get the hint today that he wanted to make out with a decked up 'me' and dance to the song 'Tip Tip Barsa Pani' like Akshay Kumar and Raveena Tandon in the rain and perform some naughty moves! But after all, our lives are not that burning or wet, so instead, I slept doing a bum to bum, as I often do in revenge when he comes home drunk. My night went quite at peace without any hiccups, whatsoever!

13

A Very Good Morning

by Swathi Umashankar

Another hurried morning, and it looked like I might just again be late. I hated being late for my early morning karate classes. It's the favourite part of my day; the intense workout gives me a high like nothing else. However, this week, I hadn't been able to get up at 5 am like I always did. Slept late, woke up late. Far too many toxic thoughts troubling my mind.

It was sheer drudgery, to get myself out of my bed and to go to the bathroom. Fifteen minutes later, I came out and got dressed. It was ten minutes to six; now how on earth was I supposed to make it to the class that fast? After all, I had to walk almost 2 km to get there, courtesy of my dysfunctional bike. I got out of my house, and trudged onwards to my class, half asleep. Thinking back, it was nothing short of a miracle that I didn't come under anyone's wheel.

It was 6:15 am, by the time I made it to the bus stop just around the corner from the practice centre. Last night had been the worst; constantly kept awake by nightmares of losing my loved ones or just completely losing out in life. The various misgivings of my past had destroyed all my sang –froid. I took a seat at the stop, not wanting to announce myself late again and get scolded for the "nth time". Just thought that I would sit and rest myself till 7 am. I honestly don't know when I fell asleep. To me, what seemed a few minutes later, I was rudely awakened. A middle-aged woman, two policemen, and a BMTC representative surrounded me. I was sleepy and utterly flabbergasted as to why I couldn't sit at a bus stop if I wished to. They pulled my knapsack from me and spilt out its contents. Out fell a pair of nunchucks, a metal chain, some ground mica, a pre-paid phone, and some money. One policeman started to question me vociferously, as to why I had such suspicious objects with me. He was not ready to listen to my explanation that I was on my way to class, sitting at the stop was merely a reprieve for me.

The other officer now came forward and told me that the middle-aged woman was a cleaner at the bus station. She had been observing my suspicious behaviour for quite some time. When I mentioned to them that I had been here only for a short while, they were bemused and showed the clock, which said 8 am. Oh my lord! The woman said I had been muttering throughout my sleep, about crime and punishment. Evidently, to her, with my haggard face and unkempt looks, I seemed nothing short of a terrorist. She had immediately called her supervisor, who promptly informed the police. This explained my current predicament.

The police stated her claim to be undisputable and marched me onward to the supervisor's office. They proceeded to frisk me there. On my person, they found a pocket knife. Along with my other possessions, they bagged and tagged that as well. By now I was fully alert and aware of what further steps they would take. I pulled an officer to my side and told him that I am a student of the Indian Karate

Academy, that I had forgotten my belt at home but I could take them to the centre and prove it to them. He rolled his eyes and paid no heed to me. I pleaded with them to reason; I vehemently stated that I was not a terrorist. It fell upon deaf ears. They'd gone through my contacts and on finding names like Ahmed Bhai and the master of death, confirmed that I was dangerous and had to be locked away till they could discern my identity. Oh, how was I to explain to them that those were the names of my gardener and my DJ friend? They just refused all my claims.

No matter how much I screamed at them, that I was a law-abiding citizen of India, my name, my contact details; nothing sank in those thick heads of theirs. They were bent upon jailing me that very instant. To them, I was a troublemaker of the highest degree, an organizer of terror attacks, or maybe even a suicide bomber. By now, a large crowd had gathered around the building. All were curious to know which "evil mastermind" had been captured by the lacklustre police. Just then, a call came to an officer and he went out to answer it. He returned a minute later, announcing with glee that the director-general of police would be arriving soon to question me. I would be escorted to jail immediately. It was very hard to fathom these series of events, so dreamlike. I threw myself on the chair, in disgust and frustration, at these ambitious clowns.

It was then a small card fell out of my clothes. A card stating that I was a brown belt member of the Indian Karate Academy. Ha! Now surely, this was solid proof of my innocence. It had my photograph, my address, and my credentials and behind it, was my registration with the police. I was elated. Not many know that a serious practitioner of karate is required to report himself/herself as one who is at such and such level of the form. Oh ho! Now, all that was needed was to get these imbeciles to go through their records, and I could go scot-free. I immediately got up and asked them to take me to jail. All were surprised by my sudden complacency with the situation they had fabricated, but far too happy for any kind of suspicion. So we went, the woman, the police, and I, to the police station.

At the station, the DG was eagerly awaiting our arrival. My shoddy appearance renewed his vigour, as he intently listened to his subordinates and the foolish woman. Meanwhile, I sat on a bench and bided my time. Soon enough his attention turned to me. He started questioning me, asking me what plan of mass destruction I had in mind. I had to struggle with each answer, to not burst out laughing at the incompetence of all who were present. The questioning got intense, my head began to throb and I was very hungry. I got up and asked the DG to go through the police records for karate practitioners in this locality. He thought I was being smart with him and rose to strike me. I, who had been expecting this, sprang back. Politely, I asked him again, to go through his records. I even offered to spend my whole life in jail, if he could not find my name on that list. My conviction must have reached him, for he opened the book and looked for my name. On reaching the third page, his face became a beautiful shade of red. I started to grin from ear to ear.

With profuse apologies, he offered to buy me breakfast. Everyone present there was baffled as to what had just occurred. They began questioning the DG, who snapped at them to stay quiet. He told them that they had made a most terrible mistake and he was furious with them. They were at a loss for words. Chuckling, I accepted his offer and we left the station. While we were on the last step, I saw the second officer peep into the book. His countenance flushed purple, and he gave a small chuckle. For he had come to know, that I was innocent after all: and the best part being, the person who had registered me three years back was the DG. What a case of "much ado about nothing". It was a good thing that the press the DG had called, turned up late eh?

ACKNOWLEDGMENTS

A big thank you to Tanishk Singh and Utkarsh Khanna for their constant guidance and support throughout, starting from the day the idea for 'A Jar Full of Joys' was conceived.

Special thanks and tight hugs to all my co-authors for contributing their time and effort to this anthology. It wouldn't have been possible without you all.

Last but not the least, you, the reader, thank you very much for picking up this book and giving us a chance to share our stories. I on behalf of the whole team behind 'A Jar Full of Joys' express my gratitude for your love and trust.

Keep smiling and Be Happy!

Namita Das

Meet the
Co-Authors

Anand Sharan

Anand Sharan has been associated with writing short notes and anecdotes. He already has a WhatsApp Group and other platforms such as Yammer where he usually shares his anthologies of daily life and happenings in and around. He has been appreciated in his community sphere. He used to work as a Telecom Engineer currently and enjoys writing anthologies for the various platforms in his firm too during his leisure times. You may also refer to his Instagram account @anand.sharan508.

Susan Bowman

Susan Bowman is a 67-year-old retired scientist. Happily living alone she enjoys gardening, reading, and contributes to an open mic event where she reads her poetry. Home is in the West Midlands area of England and with easy access to the centre of many cities, she can enjoy the theatre for ballet and opera which she enjoys. She has been writing all her life but only recently submitting her work for publication. She has had a poem accepted for an anthology to support the NHS in the UK and a crime story with a difference has been included in an anthology by Carrick Publishing. She has recently finished writing her first novel and already has plans for a second.

Rashi Sadhu

Rashi Sadhu is a Financial Planner and Content Writer. She's on a mission to spread financial literacy. She believes financial freedom should be a vital goal for every common person. Her passion involves writing poetry on real scenarios. She is a proud mother and writer (by choice). Connect with her on Twitter @RashiSadhu

Deepti L. Sharma

Dr. Deepti L. Sharma holds a Ph.D. in ecology and runs her environmental consultancy firm, but her heart lies firmly in writing. So to summarize her in one sentence – She's Married to Science, Romancing Literature!

Neha Prashar Verma

Neha is a business developer, a blogger, a traveller, a military wife and an aspiring author. In her journey from writing Market research reports to writing stories, blogs and poems, she has created various pearls with her literary skills. She loves to read in solace with her thoughts. Her works are inspired by daily life, emotions, fiction, and travels. She is a loving mother and loves music and painting.

Nivedita Karmaran

Nivedita Karmaran belongs to Mumbai, the city of dreams. While working in the field of Human Resources for a corporate company, she pursues her dream of writing stories on various writing platforms and has taken part in several anthologies. She has recently published her book on Amazon Kindle called 'On A Journey Of Life'. She has a keen interest in screenplay writing. She is enthusiastic about her micro tales, quotes which you will find on her Instagram handle @niveditakarmaran. You can also follow her blog - nivipooh@blogspot.com.

Vaishali Chandorkar Chitale

An alumna of the Indian Institute of Mass Communication, New Delhi, Vaishali Chandorkar Chitale, is an English (Hons) graduate from Hindu College, Delhi University. She is a freelance journalist, author, and poet. Her stories have been published in paperback anthologies, e-books; on Story Mirror and Bonobology. She has taught English in many schools and retired from Delhi Public school, Pune in 2004, after a career of over 14 years to follow her passion for writing. You can follow her on her blog: www.anenviablejourney.wordpress.com. She can be reached at vchandorkar@gmail.com

Priyanka Sahi

Priyanka Sahi is a full-time German Language Translator who loves to travel and explore new places in her free time. She has been an avid reader all her life but her love for writing began when she started writing travel blogs to help fellow travellers plan  their trips. She already has one completed novel and an ongoing novel on Wattpad. She is also a part-time photographer but her passion lies in writing.

Vishakha Naware

 Vishakha Naware is a typical working mom, juggling work and family. A German language trainer by profession, her passion lies in languages, reading and writing short stories. A self-proclaimed Master-Chef, she loves to travel and explore new places and cultures. In her *me*-time, she binge-watches series on Netflix and likes to get lost in the world of books.

Shaikh Abdul Wasee

Abdul likes to call himself a nobody who is trying to be somebody. He is a writer by circumstances, not by choice. You can connect with him on shaikhwasee85047@gmail.com or Instagram at @the_devoted_savage or @just_a_word_addict.

Anita Gonsalves

Anita Gonsalves is a graduate in History and English Literature and a post-graduate in History. She had lost her job due to COVID however, being a fighter she decided to pursue her favourite hobby of writing short stories and articles and had completed a course in Content Writing. Rather than concentrating on her loss, she has channelized her energy to learn something new and appreciates the quality time she gets to spend with her family. A firm believer that good times are ahead this is her first-ever story and hopefully not the last.

Arundhati Sahoo

Arundhati Sahoo is a management grad, whose heart beats for literature while she crunches numbers in excel sheets. She is the author of Identity: A mere play of gender, status, and aesthetics; which talks about a eunuch and prostitute's exploration of identity, and The Liberating Fetters, which is a collection of poems depicting thoughts of a young girl while she grows. Her bookstagram handle is @arundhati1402. She loves to interact with the literary community, so you can always drop in a message with feedback and comments.

Swathi Umashankar

Swathi Umashankar is an IT consultant, a job she thought she wouldn't have in a million years! When not clickety-clacking on the laptop, she can be found in the company of her two special men (ahem, cats) Sebastian & Lucifer. She  has recently taken up writing again after realizing her love of engaging storytelling and hopes that it will lead to a kinder and happier world for all. You can reach her at her Insta handle @Pithy_Please and follow her on her Podcast "Pithy Please" and catch up with her on her blog at PithyPlease.com. Pretty please?!!

INKFEATHERS PUBLISHING

India's Most Author Friendly Publishing House

Stay updated about latest books, anthologies, events, exclusive offers, contests, product giveaways and other things that we do to support authors.

 @Inkfeathers Publishing

 @InkfeathersPublishing

 @_Inkfeathers

 @Inkfeathers

 Inkfeathers.com

We'd love to connect with you!